The Kite Flyer

ROSE TREMAIN

A Phoenix Paperback

The Kite Flyer first published in *The Garden of the Villa Mollini*
by Hamish Hamilton in 1987
and in paperback by Sceptre
A Shooting Season and *Words With Marigold* first published
in *The Colonel's Daughter* by Hamish Hamilton in 1984
and in paperback by Sceptre.

Sinclair-Stevenson publish *The Collected Short Stories* in 1996.

This edition published in 1996 by Phoenix
a division of Orion Books Ltd
Orion House, 5 Upper St Martin's Lane, London WC2H 9EA

ISBN 1 85799 764 6

Typeset by Deltatype Ltd, Ellesmere Port, Cheshire
Printed in Great Britain by Clays Ltd, St Ives plc

CONTENTS

The Kite Flyer

In my captors' glossless eyes do I see an envious-
ness of the lustre in mine own.
   – from the Prison Treatise of Anna of Didsmill 1643

Very often, when Olivia Kingswell spoke encourag-
ingly or chidingly to herself, she addressed herself as
'my dear'. 'Pick up the pieces, my dear.' 'Don't make a
spectacle of yourself, my dear.'

Then, on a certain day, a Sunday in early summer, she
decided to break this habit. 'You are Olivia,' she told her
bulgy blue eyes in the hall mirror, 'it's as simple as that.'
And she felt amazed, as she went to the kitchen to baste the
Sunday joint, that she'd been so polite, so over-polite to
herself for so long. 'It's ridiculous!' she sniffed.

On the same Sunday, her husband, Anthony Kingswell,
as he sat and waited for his beef and potatoes, felt cold. The
coal scuttle in the sitting room was empty. He took it out to
the coal bunker and filled it up, fetched dry kindling from
the woodshed and made a fire. It was May. The light
coming in to the Kingswells' sitting room was so glaring
that the colours of Anthony's fire looked feeble. He knelt

over it, holding out his hands.

Olivia, her apron on, her nose pink from the hot kitchen, came in. She had the carriage of a Great Dane, Anthony thought, stately but bounding. Today, on his knees, he felt small beside his wife.

'Darling,' she said, 'what are you doing?'

'Trying to warm up,' he said.

'It's *May*,' said Olivia.

'I know it's May,' said Anthony.

Sunday was usually the day when Anthony Kingswell felt warmest, happiest and most close to God.

For nine years, as Vicar of the Church of St Barnabas, Didsmill, he had thought of Sunday as 'belonging' to him. This wasn't arrogance, it was simply a reaffirmation, as the Church years succeeded one another, that he had chosen the right profession. Walking, in early light, from the vicarage gate to the vestry door, smelling damp yew, touching the iron cold of the latch, he would feel God slumbering in his blood. Then, robing for Communion, as old Tom Willis tugged out with leathery hands a funereal clang from the bell, his cheeks would start to become rosy with Jesus, his fingernails pink and shiny with Jesus, and at his throat would wait the syllables of praise and thanksgiving for the knowledge that God was now wide awake in his body. Even in the depths of winter, Anthony was warm on Sundays. He could have given January sermons in his underwear. He'd look out at his meagre congregation, hunched up in overcoats and scarves and woolly hats and think, Poor things, I hold up the chalice to their lips and they sip, and yet they're chilly. What a sad coldness this must be.

Now, on this Sunday in May, the second Sunday before Whitsun, here was Anthony lighting a fire and kneeling in front of it and shivering. He knew it had been growing in him for some weeks, this awful feeling of being cold. In the same way, Olivia's awareness that she had been too polite, too evasive a person had been growing in her for about the same number of weeks, though neither Olivia nor Anthony could have said for precisely how long. However, these things were happening: God was slipping out of Anthony's veins, Olivia had learned the rightness, the sternness and the beauty, even, of her Christian name.

Though she was a conscientious vicar's wife – efficient at fund-raising, gentle-voiced, an enthusiastic maker of bramble jelly – Olivia had never been very curious about faith. She saw it as something Anthony possessed and always would, and which she didn't and never would, like a penis. It neither worried her, nor made her envious. What she had acknowledged – until recently, until she made one of the great discoveries of her life – was that her life lacked purpose. She would sit at Matins and watch her husband mount his pulpit, and know that Anthony and the Church of England were like the desert traveller and his camel, self-sufficient in the midst of emptiness, going patiently on from one small oasis to another. Olivia never yearned for her own camel. She got on with the years. One of the things she loved most about life was discovering the past. She often felt that without her local library she would have been a rather morose woman, but history made her excitable. And then, quite by chance, among the red and green and brown spines of the seventeenth century, she discovered Anna of Didsmill Wold.

One of the questions never asked by those later involved in the 'case' of Anthony and Olivia Kingswell was 'Why did Anna of Didsmill inspire Olivia in the way she did?' The answer (or at least *part* of the answer) lay in the fact that Anna was not only a martyr to her cause and a woman of action, she was also the eldest daughter of a country schoolmaster (as was Olivia), she was born on July 16th, 1620 (exactly three hundred and fourteen years to the day before Olivia), and is known, in prison, to have asked her captors for a dish of greengages, Olivia's favourite fruit. Thus, it was immediately clear to Olivia that she shared much 'common ground' with Anna. Part of this 'common ground' was the actual earth on which they both walked – the lanes, the fields and the wold of Didsmill. As Olivia's hands turned the pages of Anna's history, they trembled.

To summarise for those who do not know of her, Anna of Didsmill was born into a moderately poor Puritan family five years before the accession of Charles I. At the age of twenty-two, shepherding her father's flock of pupils into the school yard one August morning in 1642, Anna heard the voice of her stern God coming out of the school-house weathercock. The voice told her to emulate the Maid of

Orleans, to don a soldier's uniform and help bring victory to the Protestant cause against the King.

That same night, wearing her brother's clothes, she rode secretly to Fenny Stratford, where Cromwell was camped, and two months later she was fighting with his army at Edge Hill. During the battle, she fell from her horse and was captured by the Royalists. In prison, her identity as a woman was quickly revealed. She was abused by her guards, raped and tortured. She was tried for treason, found guilty and hung at Didsmill gibbet. While in prison, she wrote (and smuggled out) a treatise on the wrong she had suffered at the hands of men, exemplifying all the evils and degradations society metes out to women. Thus, she was both a woman of action and a reformer. Yet historians had neglected her. She languished in Olivia's library in one small book. Olivia rescued her. She gave a talk to the Didsmill and Didsborn W.I. about her. She discovered the cottage where she'd lived and the site of the old schoolhouse (burned down in 1805) where she heard God's voice. Slowly, yet persuasively, Anna was entering Olivia's mind. And one day, Olivia walked on the downland where the gibbet had once stood. She knew there would be no trace of it. On the exact spot where Anna of Didsmill had died, there was an aircraft hangar and the land for six miles around it was a criss-cross of runways and concrete barracks. It was an American airbase. It was rumoured that missile silos were going to be built here.

Olivia put her hands up to the perimeter fence and

imagined that this woman of long ago spoke to her in the sighing of the wire: 'Do what you can,' the voice said kindly.

If it was quite easy, then, to understand why Olivia Kingswell found a new direction of her life through her discovery of Anna of Didsmill Wold, it was much more difficult to determine (and remember, these two events went on simultaneously) why Anthony Kingswell began to lose his faith.

On this May Sunday, when he lit his feeble fire, Anthony was fifty-four years old and had held his faith in a forgiving and accessible God for more than twenty years. He had entered the Church at the age of thirty-three, the age of Christ's death. (He liked the events of his life to reverberate.) He had never regretted it. He had always imagined his faith would last him out. God was tangible to Anthony. When he snuffled on his pipe, he felt God in the embers and in his saliva. When he dreamed about his boyhood, he saw God in that space of bony flesh between the hem of his flannel shorts and the turnover of his grey socks.

You might suggest that, because he was a man who felt God to be so much a part of the physical world, he was bound to feel the presence of God diminishing as his middle age advanced. Though a good preacher, he wasn't a truly spiritual man. His faith was instinctive, not cerebral. And this fact seemed, in part, to explain what was happening. For some reason, his mind, his rational self had started to question or at least to worry about, the existence of God. Being the man he was, he sought to reassure himself by finding God in His usual places – in his pipe embers, in the dry, sweet smell of the altar rail, in the vicarage garden, and most of all in his own blood. So when he found that he felt cold, it was natural that he also felt afraid.

The vicarage, where Anthony and Olivia had lived for nine years, was a solid, Victorian, well-ordered house. Olivia managed it well, yet inhabited it lightly, keeping a careful distance from Anthony's study, which, as visiting parishioners usually sensed, was the only 'serious' room in the house. It had never been suggested that Olivia might occupy a 'serious' room of her own. 'For what?' Anthony would have asked. 'To write the W.I. Newsletter in?'

But then, after Olivia had discovered Anna, she began to have a recurring dream in which she walked aimlessly through her house, topping up the flower water, polishing coasters, plumping cushions, readying each room for someone else, always for someone else, till her own presence in the house became as faded as chintz and the rooms were like lazy strangers, just sitting about, offering nothing. So she turned a guest room into her 'serious' room. She removed the bed. She bought a cheap desk, a filing cabinet and a worklamp. Bookshelves were put up. She took down the chintz at the window. She put *A Life of Anna of Didsmill*, alone as yet, in place on the new bookshelves.

Anthony came and stared at these changes and stared at

of the window into the June wind.

Unluckily for Anthony, this particular summer was cool. Sunlight on the garden, particularly sunlight on the grey-green poplar leaves, shivering, flashing, he imagined as 'God's currency'. He loved to sit in a comfortable chair, his eyes two thin slits just open on this glory. But, in June, there didn't seem to be many glorious days. The sky was moody. Anthony looked up at the sunless blanket and said, 'Why, oh my Redeemer, have you hidden your coinage from your servant?' Then he glanced at the window of Olivia's study, wide open. She worked on, oblivious of weather. She had a title for an article, she told Anthony: *Anna of Didsmill, A Heroine for Today*. If the article was published, she would try to gather enough material for a book. When she talked about these things, her bulgy eyes were wide, like a child's eyes open on her first sight of the sea. And Anthony shuddered. How well he recognised that shining light. He had grown used to finding it, many times a week, in his own face in the mirror. '*I* used to be the one!' he wanted to say to his wife. 'I should be the one!'

It was Monday. Anthony walked in from the garden. On Monday evenings Anthony always held a 'surgery' for his parishioners. Today, the thought of the surgery appalled him. He needed to receive advice, not give it.

He poured himself a glass of sherry and sat down in the sitting room. He held his glass up to the light, and stared at the liquid. One of his most secret ways of finding God was 9 in sherry. He lit his pipe, warming his hands on the bowl. The warm pipe, the cold, strong sherry, he calmed himself with these, filling and refilling his glass and muttering peculiar prayers as, upstairs, Olivia worked on.

Not long after this Monday (Anthony had been too ill with his sherry drinking to hold his surgery and the people who came talked to Olivia instead), Olivia declared that Anna had 'instructed' her to make a trip to Greenham Common.

Anthony stared at his wife.

'No, Olivia,' he said.

She stared back at him. Colossal she seemed. A warrior. She's becoming a man, Anthony thought.

'I'm sorry, Anthony darling,' she said, 'I'm just *telling* you that I am going to Greenham on my birthday, July 16th. I am not asking for permission.'

'I can't have it,' said Anthony, 'a vicar's wife simply must not take part in this kind of political antic.'

'It's not an antic,' said Olivia, 'and anyway, churchmen and politicians are more closely linked over the question of peace than over any other, as you yourself should be aware.'

And she strode out of the kitchen where they had been eating supper and bounded upstairs to her study. Anthony heard the key turn in the lock, got up from the table, went to the Welsh dresser which, since Olivia's mother's death in 1971, had proudly displayed a Wedgewood dinner service, took down five plates and a gravy boat and smashed them on the stone floor. Olivia did not come down. He took up two more plates and hurled them at the chimneybreast. Olivia unlocked her door, ran down the stairs and into the kitchen and hit her husband in the face. He sat down among the broken china and started to cry. Olivia stared at him, disgusted. Children! she thought scornfully. Men are *children*! But then, he reached out for her hands and held them to his face. 'Help me, Olivia,' he sobbed. 'I'm losing Jesus.'

Olivia postponed the trip to Greenham. Instead, Canon Stapleton (whose reply to Anthony's Trinity letter had been vague and dismissive) was persuaded by Olivia to come and stay with them. The weather brightened in July, and Anthony and Canon Stapleton went for long walks in the Didsmill beechwoods. 'Something,' said Stapleton to Anthony, 'has made you angry with God. That's all. You're angry with Him and through your anger you've lost Him. If you can remember *why* you're angry with Him, then you'll be able to forgive Him and beg His forgiveness and you will find him again. Tiffs with God are more normal than you imagine.'

On they walked, under the green fanlights of beech, and Anthony listened and felt hope revive. But, search as he tried, he simply couldn't remember why he was angry with God. He knew why he was angry with Olivia, but he couldn't remember why he was angry with God, or even if he *was* angry, and after some days, Canon Stapleton had to return to Winchester and at his departure Anthony felt invaded by despair.

That same day, Olivia's outline for her article was accepted by *History in Perspective*, a monthly history magazine. As Olivia showed Anthony the letter, her eyes were luminous with joy. He stared morosely past her, so envious of her happiness he couldn't utter. She smiled. She crowed. 'I'm determined there'll be a book,' she said.

'Beware of pride,' he muttered and handed her back the letter. A look of disbelief crossed her face. 'Anthony,' she said breathlessly, 'this quarrel of yours with God, please don't turn it into a quarrel with me!'

You might say that the events described so far represented the 'first stage' in the odd case of Anthony and Olivia Kingswell. From this point, they entered the 'second stage' or 'second act', if you like, of what some would later describe as a tragedy.

The second stage really began that night when, lying in the dark beside his wife, Anthony Kingswell stumbled on the notion that it was Olivia who was responsible for God's withdrawal from him, that it was Olivia who, by seeking to change the natural order of things with her wretched Martyr of Didsmill, was deflecting God away from him and towards herself.

This was a strangely irrational decision for Anthony to come to. No one knew better than Anthony that Olivia's faith was, at best, peripheral to her life. She'd always been happy to let him be the believer and had certainly never shown any sign of wanting to get closer to God than she already was. This, however, Anthony decided as he lay and looked at his wife's sleeping body, must have been a deliberate deception. She must have been envious of his faith for years and waited, waited for her chance to deflect it . . .

Without waking Olivia, Anthony got out of bed and went down to his study. Outside the window, he could hear the cry of a nightingale and he felt more at peace, more assuaged than he'd felt for months. He reached for his bible and turned to the *Epistle of Paul to the Ephesians*, Chapter 5, verse 24: . . . *as the Church is subject unto Christ, so let the wives be to their husbands in every thing.*

Then, in his neat and rather beautiful writing, he wrote out these words on a card, tiptoed to the kitchen and propped the card up on the Welsh dresser in the exact place where the gravy boat used to stand. He breathed deeply. He could sense, through the Venetian blind, the approach of dawn and he knelt and prayed: 'In the coming of morning let me feel you again, my true and only God. Like a lover who runs to the shore as the sails of his beloved are glimpsed on the horizon, let me run to meet you in the sunrise and find you there.' He stayed in his attitude of prayer, with his chin on the kitchen table, till he could feel the room fill with soft, yellowy light. Olivia, in her dressing-gown, found him like this and touched his head gently. 'Come back to bed, Anthony. It's only half past five,' she said. And he opened his eyes. It seemed to him that in the split second before Olivia touched him, he had felt it near him, waiting, the Holy Spirit. In another moment, as the kitchen filled with the dawn, it would have entered him.

'You prevented it!' he cried, and turned upwards to his wife a face of stone.

Not long after this, Olivia went to Greenham.

Courage in the midst of desolation had always moved her. She had remembered all her life a story her schoolmaster father had told her about a tribe of American Indians called the Ram Tiku, whose sacred valley had been destroyed by lumberjacks. Generations of these Indians, living now on dry, difficult earth, sent their braves in to reclaim the valley, until there were no young men left and the valley became a shrine in the mind, not a place anyone could remember. The perseverance of the Greenham women reminded Olivia of the perseverance of the Ram Tiku. The American soldiers had the tough, beefy faces of lumberjacks. The women's 'benders' were like polythene tepees. And life – such as it could be there – congregated round little fires. Drinking Bovril, Olivia told a group of young women (some of their faces were like the painted faces of braves) the story of Anna of Didsmill. They listened eagerly. 'Didsmill,' said a stern-browed woman called Josie, 'we must start thinking about Didsmill. Next year they're building silos there.'

The group round Olivia grew. Someone gave her a helping of bean stew on a plastic plate.

'You know,' said Olivia, 'if Anna had been on the side of the King, as Joan of Arc was on the side of her King, she would have become a heroine, a saint perhaps. It's what side you're on that matters. I've understood this now.'

There was rueful laughter. Olivia looked round at the squatting women spooning up their stew. 'Forgive me,' she wanted to say to them. 'Forgive me my sheltered life. It's going to change.'

'I would really like,' she said at length, looking round at the camp, with its mud and its urban litter, 'to help begin something at Didsmill. I think it's going to become an important place.'

It was a warm but windy day. On the Didsmill downland the wind was fierce as Anthony came out of the vicarage, hurled his home-made kite into the car and drove fast to the rolling hills above the Didsmill base.

Here, he got out and threw his head back and imagined, under the white bellies of the clouds, the earth turning. He felt a sudden lightness. His spirits lifted. He gathered up his kite and started to run with it, playing the string out behind him. It was an insubstantial thing and it began to lift almost at once. Anthony stopped running and held the taut line. He'd made kites since he was a boy, dragon kites, aeroplane kites, seagull kites. He knew how to handle them. And today's wind was perfect. The kite was white and he watched it turn and dance, turn and dance, then stream off higher, tearing at the string. He ran with it again. It was almost at the limit of the strong nylon line now and

Anthony felt weightless, so full of the spirit of the kite he almost believed he could follow it aloft, up and up into the fathomless blue . . . And then he saw what he hoped would happen: half a mile above him, the kite began to break up. The white paper sheets were torn from the fragile frame and came flying down to earth like a scatter of leaves. Anthony watched them fall, the twenty-three white pages of Olivia's article, he watched them scatter and tear and go flying off over the curves of the hill. The kite string was limp in his hand and he was breathing hard. 'Beautiful . . .' he murmured. And he knelt.

So she returned from Greenham to find her article (of which she had made no duplicate) gone.

'Where is it, Anthony?' she said, patiently.

'On the downs,' he said from the depths of his pillows.

Returning from the kite flying, he had lain down exhausted on his bed and slept, and when he woke the exhaustion was still there and he slept again, and now he felt entombed in the bed and couldn't move. He was pale and his eyes were hectic. He's going mad, Olivia thought.

He lay and stared at his room. He thought of autumn coming and then winter and he knew that his soul was filling up with ice. But it was clear to him now: the light he saw in Olivia's eyes was *his* light. She had stolen it. It was God's light and it belonged to him. Without it, he would grow colder and colder. On the windy down, destroying her article, he had stolen some of it back. For a few

16

moments, it had warmed him. But it hadn't lasted. And here was Olivia, strong as a stag beside his bed.

'I'll write it again, you know,' she said through hard, set lips and she turned and bounded from the room. His door slammed. She was without sympathy for him.

He didn't speak to her for two days and she didn't speak to him. He stayed in bed. She worked in her room. She fed him frozen pies and jelly on smeared trays she hadn't bothered to wipe. On the third day, he left her. Weak and grey, he put a small suitcase in the car and drove to Winchester, where Canon Stapleton took him in. 'All I can advise,' said Canon Stapleton, 'is some time in retreat.'

So Anthony entered Muir Priory. He was given a tiny, white room with a narrow, uncurtained window. On one of the walls was an ivory crucifix.

The second draft of Olivia's article was completed in ten days and she knew it was better than the first.

September came, dry, windy and bright. Olivia typed out the article (careful, this time, to keep a copy of it) and sent it off to *History in Perspective* and waited. While waiting, she wrote to the Greenham woman, Josie, and asked if she would come and stay with her, 'to make concrete plans for something at Didsmill'.

When she thought about Anthony, she felt cross with God. He could be so spiteful, this supposedly loving Deity. It was mean of Him to have withdrawn from Anthony's spittle. But she was aware that, among these thoughts, crouched her knowledge of her own withdrawal from her husband. He had always preferred God to her and she'd always accepted this. God was, as she'd so often imagined during Matins, Anthony's camel; she was simply the mat, frayed by desert winds, on which the rider had lain. Now, she was tired of being a mat and she folded it away. The camel lay buried in an eternity of sand. The rider was hungry, lost. The nights were cold. Olivia felt wistful, yet unmoved. She tore the card on the dresser into pieces, made up her bed with clean sheets that held no trace of the smell of Anthony. Let the men heal each other, she thought.

The vicarage, without Anthony, was very quiet. Olivia filled it with bowls of greengages and with whispered conversations to Anna. 'Anna,' she said, making sandwiches for the visit of the temporary vicar, 'I am fifty-one.'

The temporary vicar was a fat, pasty man. 'I suffer from acidity,' he said as he ate Olivia's tea.

'You know,' Olivia heard herself reply, 'I don't think I'm interested in symptoms any more, only in causes.'

The vicar belched and smiled. 'Well,' he said, wiping his mouth with his napkin, 'fishpaste is one.'

When he left, Olivia knew how glad she was to be alone. She got out the Ordnance Survey map and calculated the distance from Greenham to Didsmill. It was twenty-three miles. Anna was twenty-three when she was hung. Twenty-three pages of her treatise remained. While in prison, she wrote to her mother and father twenty-three times, asking

for forgiveness.

Then Josie arrived. She was very tired and dirty. Olivia, gentle as a mother, ran a deep bath for her in the big, old-fashioned bath, put her to bed and brought her supper on a clean tray.

In Muir Priory, away from his parish and its responsibilities, away from Olivia, Anthony began to feel calmer.

Dean Neville Scales, warden of the Priory, was a long-limbed man with a passion for gardening. He liked to preach about God in Nature. He made sure that the Priory gardens were colourful and neat, his pride and joy being a grove of Japanese acers, scarlet and gold and purple.

The first leaves were going from the acers as Anthony walked alone on the priory lawns. Dew on the springy grass: God's moisture everywhere except on his own tongue. He wetted and wetted his lips. Prayer came to him lightly, its syllables flowing freely into his mind. This was a benevolent sign. He walked and prayed and, though the contours of the garden were mirror-sharp, he felt on his forehead some warmth from the sun.

He liked the simple, stark routine of each day and he liked the emptiness of his room. When he thought about his home, it seemed like a place too cluttered with objects and with feeling. He saw Olivia in it everywhere – Olivia's light. I hate her, he thought.

To Dean Scales he confessed. 'I still feel loving kindness towards all things, or at least to most things, but not towards my wife.'

In the Dean's silence, he detected shock.

'God's ministers cannot harbour hatred,' he said, blowing his nose on a clean square of silk. 'Whatever your wife has done, you must try to forgive her.'

'I can't, Dean.'

'Are you telling me she's in mortal sin?'

'No, Dean.'

'Then your hatred is petty?'

Anthony sighed. He felt ashamed to say that his hate sprang from envy. The enviousness itself seemed, in the confessional, vain and silly, his idea that Olivia had 'stolen' God from him fanciful and stupid. He felt humble and sick. He longed, longed for some relief from his confusions.

'Let me stay here till I find God again, Dean.'

'We shall see how you progress.'

'I can't go back into the world.'

'And your responsibilities?'

'I can't honour them, till I find Jesus . . .'

'What makes you believe you will find Jesus here?'

Anthony sighed deeply. 'I must,' he said, 'or I shall go mad.'

Two weeks passed. The leaves on the gold acers were edged with brown. In everything, Anthony strove for obedience – from the cleaning of his supper plate (one evening, the Priory cook served up hamburgers and the raucous, treacherous world came teeming back into Anthony's head and made wounds in his fragile calm) to the hour-by-hour discomfort of kneeling. Each day was punctuated by fourteen 'stations of prayer', this punitive number echoing the fourteen Stations of the Cross. The first station was at five-thirty and the last at midnight. The time for sleep was short, but it was a grateful, dreamless sleep that Anthony slept. On the edge of it, in his curtainless room, he'd lie and look out at the stars and allow into his troubled head thoughts of heaven.

Josie Mecklin was a tanned, freckled woman with the patient smile of a teacher. During her stay in Olivia's house, she expected to instruct this middle-class vicar's wife on the true meaning of hardship and deprivation. But, to her surprise, she found she spent a lot of time listening to Olivia talking about martyrdom and belief. Olivia, it seemed, didn't need telling what had to be done. 'I think,' said this Great Dane, this stag of a woman, 'we are the "new Amazons".' We're middle-aged, middle-class, pampered and ignorant. But we're *strong*. We're strong because we've understood. We'll fight to the death.'

Josie stayed three days. She spent a lot of time lying in the bath. She'd talk to Olivia through the bathroom door. A plan emerged from the clouds of steam: on the anniversary of the death of Anna of Didsmill, October 3rd, two hundred women would march from Greenham to the Didsmill base. They would take candles and brushwood torches. They would arrive at Didsmill as the sun went down and hold a silent, night-long vigil at the main gate. At first light Olivia would read aloud passages from Anna's treatise. Then they would disperse peacefully, many of them to walk the twenty-three miles back to Greenham.

Olivia, sitting on a hard chair in the passage, felt her heart begin to race. No moment in her life now seemed as meaningful as this one – her marriage, the birth of her two sons, Anthony's ordination, none of these milestones had knocked with such strength on her ribs. She put a hand to her chest. 'Let me not die, God, before these things happen.'

Pink and shiny from her baths, Josie ate hungrily in Olivia's kitchen. Over cups of coffee, maps came out and a route from Greenham to Didsmill was decided on. It was also decided that Olivia would return to Greenham with Josie and spend a reciprocal three days there, talking to the women about Anna and enlisting volunteers for the Didsmill march. In her loft, Olivia found a sleeping bag used by one of her sons at scout camp. It smelt of mothballs and it had a damp, cold feel. But already, Olivia could imagine her body inside it, warming it up.

On the morning of Olivia's departure with Josie, a letter arrived from *History in Perspective*. 'Thank you,' it said, 'for your interesting and excellently researched article. We would like to offer you the sum of £150 and we will hope to include the article in our February issue.'

Olivia drew Josie's hard shoulders towards her and let her excitement crackle in an impulsive kiss on her new friend's cheek.

22   On October 2nd, God returned to take up temporary

lodging in Anthony's body.

He was in the Priory library, searching for a book Dean Scales had recommended to him, called *Nazareth and 20th Century Man*. A young curate, a withdrawn person Anthony had never spoken to, was sitting at one of the library tables. As Anthony passed him, he noticed that the curate was reading the very book Anthony had come into the library to find. Anthony stopped. He sat down opposite the curate and stared at the man's lowered head and at the book under his white hands. He felt like a supplicant. 'I have made,' he said in prayer and with a strange confusion of metaphor, 'my willow cabin at your gate, Lord. In it, I stand and wait. I serve you, but you do not come to me.' At this point in Anthony's prayer, the curate looked up at him and smiled and handed Anthony the book. The young man then got up without a word and walked out of the library. Anthony held the book to his chest. It was warm from the other man's touch. At last, at *last* a sign had been given. Tears came to his eyes. The tears were hot. With a sob of joy, he felt God streaming down his face.

Anthony left Muir Priory with the Dean's blessing on the late afternoon of the following day.

It seemed very strange to him to be driving his car. It was raining. His hands fumbled to find the windscreen wipers. The noise of the car distressed him. The houses he passed seemed ugly beyond imagining. He began to long for the beauty of his garden and the peace of his church. He was full of anxiety. The world, he thought, opposes God's habitation in me. He drove on. In the cloudy sky, the light went early and the road in front of Anthony grew pale, its contours indistinct. But as darkness came on and blotted out the landscape around him, he felt calmer.

As he neared Didsmill, the rain ceased. Anthony stopped the car on a quiet road and got out, hoping, before the world and Olivia sprang at him again, to catch a glimpse of the same stars he'd seen from his window in the Priory. But the sky was uniform black and Anthony felt disappointment change to fear. He needed reassurance. He needed a *sign*. The stars, in place above him, would have been a sign.

He was about to get back into the car, when, far along the road in front of him, yet seeming to lie exactly in the path of the car, he saw a flickering light. It was a fluid, yellowy light, moving, beckoning. 'There it is,' Anthony whispered, 'my sign.'

And he began to walk towards it. As he neared it, he saw that the light was moving across the road, not towards him as he had believed. He squinted at it. It undulated under the trees. And now there was a faint sound accompanying the light, a shuffle of feet, and Anthony knew that, far from being alone on the road as he had thought, he was with a great shapeless, hidden gathering of people.

He could see them now: a slow procession, a long, long line of marchers holding candles and torches. He stood in the shadow of the trees, hiding. He could hear hundreds of voices, whispering, laughing. Women's voices. He turned away. The lights and the voices seemed to follow him, mocking. *You took us for a sign*! He tried to pray, but all his mind would construct were the four syllables of his wife's name: O-li-vi-a!

The threads were gathering now. The ending of the story of Anthony and Olivia Kingswell was coming . . .

All night, in the dusty, unkempt house he could barely recognise as his home, Anthony sat and waited for his wife. He grew cold. A wind got up. Anthony covered himself with a blanket. He dozed in the chair and dreamed of his future: his pulpit had been rebuilt in gold; it was higher than before. From it, he looked down on the potato faces of his parishioners. 'I,' he thundered, 'am the ploughman, and I plough you into the earth!' He woke shivering and trembling. He stared at the room, ghostly now in dawn light: dead flowers on the table, dust and crumbs on the carpet, old newspapers on the arms of chairs, boxes of leaflets piled up where a vase pedestal used to stand . . .

When she came in at last, the room was filled with sunlight and she wasn't alone. She stared at him. The woman at her back stared at him.

'Anthony,' she said coldly, 'why didn't you let me know you were coming back?' And she crossed the room and kissed him and he could feel her hard forehead against his, bruising him.

He said nothing. She pulled away and looked at him. So thin, he is, was her thought. 'This is Josie,' she said, and the 25 woman smiled. Anthony pushed the blanket off his body and stood up. He was freezing.

'There's a fine wind, Olivia,' he said. 'Let's go for a walk together. We can take a kite.'

Sleep, thought Olivia. I have never wanted sleep so much as I want it now. But she agreed to go with him. Later, she would sleep.

As she went out with Anthony, she heard Josie upstairs, running a bath and Olivia knew that, tired as she was, she was at last happy in her life.

But the life of Olivia Kingswell had only minutes – twenty-three minutes exactly – to last.

Anthony didn't drive to the downs. He drove to a potato field, a large field spread round a deep pond, muddy and grim in its recent harvest, with a few rotting potatoes left among the cut stalks. Here, with his nylon kite string strong as wire, he strangled Olivia and threw her body into the pond. The body didn't sink, but lay bobbing on the surface and the algae, displaced by its fall, reformed around it. Anthony felt the sour taste of this green, elemental weed on his tongue and vomited into the mud. Out of his mouth came pouring the chewed and mangled pieces of the body of Christ.

Olivia's murder, when it became known, caught the public interest for some time. 'Why?' the people asked. '*Why* did he kill her?' But after the trial, it was quite soon forgotten. Even the question *why*, never answered to counsel's satisfaction, was forgotten and Anthony started on his six year prison sentence in the same way as he had started on his Priory retreat – with a frail kind of hope.

God, however, did seem to have left him, and the only feelings of wonder he ever experienced again were on windy days. He taught some of his prison colleagues how to make kites out of coat-hanger wire, newspaper and paste, and when the wind bellowed round the prison walls, these things could be seen dancing above the exercise yard. In the tug of their strings, Anthony could feel the pull of heaven.

A Shooting Season

'You're writing a *what*?'
   'A novel.'
Looking away from him, nervously touching her hair, Anna remembered, the last time I saw him my hair wasn't grey.
   'Why the hell are you writing a novel?'
Grey hairs had sprouted at forty-one. Now, at forty-five, she sometimes thought, my scalp is exhausted, that's all, like poor soil.
   'I've wanted to write a novel ever since I was thirty. Long before, even . . .'
   'You never told me.'
   'No. Of course not.'
   'Why "of course not"?'
   'You would have laughed, as you're laughing now.'
Anna had always been enchanted by his laugh. It was a boy's giggle; (you climbed a cold dormitory stairway and heard it bubble and burst behind a drab door!) yet their son didn't have it: at sixteen, he had the laugh of a rowdy man.
   'I don't approve.'
28   'No.'

'It's an act of postponed jealousy.'

Well, if so, then long postponed. Six years since separation; four since the divorce and his remarriage to Susan, the pert blonde girl who typed his poems. And it wasn't jealousy, surely? In learning to live without him, she had taught herself to forget him utterly. If she heard him talk on the radio, she found herself thinking, his cadences are echoing Dylan Thomas these days, he's remembered how useful it is, if you happen to be a poet, also to be Welsh. Three years older than her, he had come to resemble a Welsh hillside – craggy outcrop of a man, unbuttoned to weather and fortune, hair wiry as gorse. Marcus. Fame clung to his untidy look. No doubt, she thought, he's as unfaithful to Susan as he was to me.

'How did it start?'

The novel-writing, he meant, but he had a way, still, of sending fine ripples through the water of ordinary questions which invited her to admit: I was in love with him for such a long time that parting from him was like a drowning. When I was washed ashore, the sediment of him still clogged me.

'I found there were things I wanted to say.'

'Oh, there always were!'

'Yes, but stronger now. Before I get old and start forgetting.'

'But a *novel*?'

'Why not?'

'You were never ambitious.'

No. Not when she was his: Mrs Marcus Ridley, wife of   29

the poet. Not while she bore his children and made rugs while he wrote and they slept.

'Do your pockets still have bits of sand in them?'

He laughed, took her strong wrist and held her hand to his face. 'I don't know. No one empties them for me.'

*

Anna had been at the rented cottage for three weeks. A sluggish river flowed a few yards from it: mallard and moorhen were the companions of her silence, the light of early morning was silver. In this temporary isolation, she had moved contentedly in her summer sandals, setting up a work table in the sunshine, another indoors by the open fire. Her novel crept to a beginning, then began to flow quietly like the river. She celebrated each day's work with two glasses, sometimes more, of the home-made wine she had remembered to bring with her. She slept well with the window wide open on the Norfolk sky. She dreamed of her book finished and bound. Then one morning Margaret, her partner in her craft business, telephoned. The sound of the telephone ringing was so unfamiliar that it frightened her. She remembered her children left on their own in London; she raced to answer the unforeseen but now obvious emergency. But no, said Margaret, no emergency, only Marcus.

'Marcus?'

'Yes. Drunk and full of his songs. Said he needed to see you.'

'And you told him where I was?'

'Yes. He said if I didn't, he'd pee on the pottery shelf.'

*

'Marcus.'

The rough feel of his face was very familiar; she might have touched it yesterday. She thought suddenly, for all his puerile needs, he's a man of absolute mystery; I never understood him. Yet they had been together for ten years. The Decade of the Poet she called it, wanting to bury him with formality and distance. And yet he surfaced in her: she seldom read a book without wondering, how would Marcus have judged that? And then feeling irritated by the question. On such occasions, she would always remind herself: he doesn't even bother to see the children, let alone me. He's got a new family (Evan 4, Lucy 3) and they, now, take all his love – the little there ever was in him to give.

'You look so healthy, Anna. Healthy and strong. I suppose you always were strong.'

'Big-boned, my mother called it.'

'How is your mother?'

'Dead.'

'You never let me know.'

'No. There was no point.'

'I could have come with you – to the funeral or whatever.'

'Oh, Marcus . . .'

'Funerals are ghastly. I could have helped you through.'

'Why don't you see the children?'

He let her hand drop. He turned to the window, wide open on the now familiar prospect of reed and river. Anna noticed that the faded corduroy jacket he was wearing was stretched tight over his back. He seemed to have outgrown it.

'Marcus . . . ?'

He turned back to her, hands in his pockets.

'No accusations. No bloody accusations!'

Oh yes, she noticed, there's the pattern: I ask a question, Marcus says it's inadmissible, I feel guilty and ashamed . . .

'It's a perfectly reasonable question.'

'Reasonable? It's a guilt-inducing, jealous, mean-minded question. You know perfectly well why I don't see the children: because I have two newer, younger and infinitely more affectionate children, and these newer, younger and infinitely more affectionate children are bitterly resented by the aforementioned older, infinitely less affectionate children. And because I am a coward.'

He should be hit, she thought, then noticed that she was smiling.

'I brought some of my home-made wine,' she said, 'it's a disgusting looking yellow, but it tastes rather good. Shall we have some?'

'Home-made wine? I thought you were a business*person*. When the hell do you get time to make wine?'

'Oh Marcus, I have plenty of time.'

Anna went to the cold, pavement-floored little room she had decided to think of as 'the pantry'. Its shelves were absolutely deserted except for five empty Nescafé jars, a dusty goldfish bowl (the debris of another family's Norfolk summer) and her own bottles of wine. It was thirty-five years since she had lived in a house large enough to have a pantry, but now, in this cupboard of a place, she could summon memories of Hodgson, her grandfather's butler, uncorking Stones ginger beer for her and her brother on timeless summer evenings – the most exquisite moments of all the summer holidays. Then, one summer, she found herself there alone. Hodgson had left. Her brother Charles had been killed at school by a cricket ball.

Anna opened a bottle of wine and took it and two glasses out to her table, in the garden, where Marcus had installed himself. He was looking critically at her typewriter and at the unfinished pages of her book lying beside it.

'You don't mean to say you're typing it?'

She put the wine and the glasses on the table. She noticed that the heavy flint she used as a paperweight had been moved.

'Please don't let the pages blow away, Marcus.'

'I'm sure it's a mistake to type thoughts directly onto paper. Writing words by hand is part of the process.'

'Your process.'

'I don't know any writers who type directly.'

'You know me. Please put the stone back Marcus.'

He replaced the pages he had taken up, put the flint down gently and spread his wide hand over it. He was looking at her face.

'Don't write about me, Anna, will you?'

She poured the wine. The sun touched her neck and she remembered its warmth with pleasure.

'Don't make me the villain.'

'There is no villain.'

She handed him the glass of wine. Out in the sunshine, he looked pale beside her. A miraculous three weeks of fine weather had tanned her face, neck and arms, whereas he . . . how did he spent his days now? She didn't know. He looked as if he'd been locked up. Yet he lived in the country with his new brood. She it was – and their children – who had stayed on in the London flat.

'How's Susan?'

No. She didn't want to ask. Shouldn't have asked. She'd only asked in order to get it over with: to sweep Susan and his domestic life to the back of her mind, so that she could let herself be nice to him, let herself enjoy him.

'Why ask?'

'To get it over with!'

He smiled. She thought she sensed his boyish laughter about to surface.

'Susan's got a lover.'

Oh damn him! Damn Marcus! Feeling hurt, feeling cheated, he thought I'd be easy consolation. No wonder the novel annoys him; he sees the ground shifting under him, sees a time when he's not the adored, successful granite he always thought he was.

'Damn the lover.'

'What?'

He'd looked up at her, startled. What he remembered most vividly about her was her permanence. The splash of bright homespun colour that was Anna: he had only to turn his head, open a door, to find her there. No other wife or mistress had been like her; these had often been absent when he'd searched for them hardest. But Anna: Anna had always *wanted* to be there.

'I'm not very interested in Susan's lover.'

'No. He isn't interesting. He's a chartered surveyor.'

'Ah. Well, reliable probably.'

'D'you think so? Reliable, are they, as a breed? He looks pitiful enough to be it. Perhaps that's what she wants.'

'And you?'

'Me?'

'What do you want, Marcus? Did you come here just to tell me your wife had a lover?'

'Accusations again. All the bloody little peeves!'

'I want to know why you came here.'

'So do I.'

'What?'

'So do I want to know. All I know is that I wanted to see you. If that's not good enough for you, I'll go away.'

Further along the river, she could hear the mallard quacking. Some evenings at sunset, she had walked through the reeds to find them (two pairs, one pair with young) and throw in scraps for them. Standing alone, the willows in front of her in perfect silhouette, she envied the ducks their sociability. No one comes near them, she thought, only me standing still. Yet they have everything – everyone – they need.

'I love it here.'

She had wanted to sit down opposite Marcus with her glass of wine, but he had taken the only chair. She squatted, lifting her face to the sun. She knew he was watching her.

'Do you want me to go away?'

She felt the intermittent river breeze on her face, heard the pages of her novel flap under the stone. She examined his question, knew that it confused her, and set it aside.

'The novel's going to be about Charlie.'

'Charlie?'

'My brother Charles. Who died at school. I'm imagining that he lived on, but not as him, as a girl.'

'Why as a girl?'

'I thought I would understand him better as a girl.'

'Will it work?'

'The novel?'

'Giving Charlie tits.'

'Yes, I think so. It also means she doesn't have to play cricket and risk being killed.'

'I'd forgotten Charlie.'

'You never knew him.'

'I knew him as a boy – through your memories. He of Hodgson's ginger beer larder!'

'Pantry.'

She's got stronger, Marcus decided. She's gone grey and

it suits her. And she's still wearing her bright colours. Probably makes not just her own clothes now, but ponchos and smocks and bits of batik to sell in her shops. And of course her son's friends fall in love with her. She's perfect for a boy: bony, maternal and sexy. Probably her son's in love with her too.

'Can I stay for dinner?'

Anna put her glass to her lips and drained it. He always, she thought, made requests sound like offers.

*

Anna scrutinised the contents of the small fridge: milk, butter, a bunch of weary radishes, eggs. Alone, she would have made do with the radishes and an omelette, but Marcus had a lion's appetite. His most potent memory of a poetry-reading fortnight in America was ordering steak for breakfast. He had returned looking ruddy, like the meat.

Anna sighed. The novel had been going well that morning. Charlie, renamed Charlotte, was perched high now above her cloistered schooldays on the windswept catwalk of a new university. Little gusts of middle-class guilt had begun to pick at her well-made clothes and at her heart. She was ready for change.

'Charlotte can wait,' Marcus told Anna, after her one feeble attempt to send him away. 'She'll be there tomorrow and I'll be gone. And anyway, we owe it to each other – one dinner.'

I owe nothing, Anna thought. No one (especially not

pretty Susan with her tumbling fair hair and her flirtatious eyes) could have given herself – her time, her energy, her love – more completely to one man than she to Marcus. For ten years he had been the landscape that held her whole existence – one scarlet poppy on the hills and crags of him, sharing his sky.

'One dinner!'

*

She took the car into Wroxham, bought good dark fillet, two bottles of Beaujolais, new potatoes, a salad and cheese.

While she was gone, he sat at the table in the sunshine, getting accustomed to the gently scented taste of her homemade wine and, despite a promise not to, reading her novel. Her writing bored him after a very few pages; he needed her presence, not her thoughts.

I've cried for you, he wanted to tell her. There have been times when – yes, several of them – times when I haven't felt comfortable with the finality of our separation, times when I've thought, there's more yet, I need more. And why couldn't you be part of my life again, on its edge? I would honestly feel troubled less – by Susan's chartered surveyor, by the coming of my forty-ninth birthday – yes, much less, if you were there in your hessian or whatever it is you wear and I could touch you. Because ten years is, after all, a large chunk of our lives, and though I never admit it, I now believe that my best poems were written during those ten and what followed has been mainly repetition. And I wanted to ask you, where are those rugs you made while I worked? Did you chuck them out? Why was the silent making of your rugs so intimately connected to my perfect arrangement of words?

*

'So here we are . . .'

The evening promised to be so warm that Anna had put a cloth on the table outside and laid it for supper. Marcus had helped her prepare the food and now they sat facing the sunset, watching the colour go first from the river, then from the willows and poplars behind it.

'Remember Yugoslavia?'

'Yes, Marcus.'

'Montenegro.'

'Yes.'

'Those blue thistles.'

'Umm.'

'Our picnic suppers!'

'Stale bread.'

'What?'

'The bread in Yugoslavia always tasted stale.'

'We used to make love in a sleeping bag.'

'Yes.'

Anna thought, it will soon be so dark, I won't be able to see him clearly, just as, in my mind, I have only the most indistinct perception of how he *is* in that hard skin, if I ever knew. For a moment she considered going indoors to get a candle, but decided it would be a waste of time; the breeze would blow it out. And the darkness suits us, suits this odd meeting, she thought. In it, we're insubstantial; we're each imagining the other one, that's all.

'I read the novel, as far as you've gone.'

'Yes. I thought you probably would.'

'I never pictured you writing.'

'No. Well, I never pictured you arriving here. Margaret told me you said you "needed" me. What on earth did you mean?'

'I think about you – often.'

'Since Susan found her surveyor?'

'That's not fair.'

'Yes, it's fair. You could have come to see me – and the children – any time you wanted.'

'I wanted . . .'

'What?'

'Not the children. You.'

For a moment, Anna allowed herself to remember: 'You, in the valley of my arms,/ my quaint companion on the mountain./ How wisely did I gather you,/ my crimson bride . . .' Then she took a sip of beaujolais and began:

'I've tried.'

'What?'

'To love other people. Other men, I mean.'

'And?'

'The feelings don't seem to last. Or perhaps I've just been unlucky.'

'Yes. You deserve someone.'

'I don't want anyone, Marcus. This is what I've at last understood. I have the children and the craft shops and one or two men friends to go out with, and now I have the novel . . .'

'I miss you, Anna.'

She rested her chin on folded hands and looked at him. Mighty is a perfect word, she thought. To me, he has always seemed mighty. And when he left me, every room, every place I went to was full of empty space. Only recently had I got used to it, decided finally to stop trying to fill it up. And now there he is again, his enormous shadow, darker, nearer than the darkness.

'You see, I'm not a poet any more.'

'Yes, you are, Marcus. I read your new volume . . .'

'No I'm not. I won't write anything more of value.'

'Why?'

'Because I'm floundering, Anna. I don't know what I expect of myself any more, as a poet or as a man. Susan's destroying me.'

'Oh rot! Susan was exactly the woman you dreamed of.'

'And now I have dreams of you.'

Anna sighed and let Marcus hear the sigh. She got up and walked the few yards to the river and watched it shine at her feet. For the first time that day, the breeze made her shiver.

*

Light came early. Anna woke astonished and afraid. 41

Marcus lay on his stomach, head turned away from her, his right arm resting down the length of her body.

A noise had woken her, she knew, yet there was nothing: only the sleeper's breath next to her and the birds tuning up, like a tiny hidden orchestra, for their full-throated day. Then she heard them: two shots, then a third and a fourth. Marcus turned over, opened his eyes and looked at her. She was sitting up and staring blankly at the open window. The thin curtains moved on a sunless morning.

'Anna . . .'

The strong hand on her arm wanted to tug her gently down, but she resisted its pressure, stayed still, chin against her knees.

'Someone's shooting.'

'Come back to sleep.'

'No, I can't. Why would someone be shooting?'

'The whole world's shooting!'

'I must go and see.'

Marcus lay still and watched Anna get up. As she pulled on a faded, familiar gown, both had the same thought: it was always like this, Anna getting up first, Marcus in bed half asleep, yet often watching Anna.

'What are you going to do?'

'I don't know. But I have to see.'

The morning air was chilly. It was sunless, Anna realised, only because the sun had not yet risen. A mist squatted above the river; the landscape was flattened and obscured in dull white. Anna stared. The dawn has extraordinary purpose, she thought, everything contained, everything shrouded by the light but emerging minute by minute into brightness and shape, so that while I stand still it all changes. She began to walk along the river. The ground under her sandals were damp and the leather soon became slippery. Nothing moved. The familiar breeze had almost died in the darkness, the willow leaves hung limp and wet. Anna stopped, rubbed her eyes.

'Where are you?'

She waited, peering into the mist. The mist was yellowing, sunlight slowly climbing. A dog barked, far off.

'Where are you?'

Senseless question. Where are you? Where are you? Anna walked on. The surface of the water, so near her slippery feet, was absolutely smooth. The sun was climbing fast now and the mist was tumbling, separating, making way for colour and contour. Where *are* you! The three words came echoing down the years. Anna closed her eyes. They came and shot the ducks, she told herself calmly. That's all. Men came with guns and had a duck shoot and the mallard are gone. When I come down here with my scraps, I won't find them. But that's all. The river flows on. Everything else is just as it was yesterday and the day before and the day before that. I am still Anna. Birds don't matter. I have a book to write. And the sun's coming up . . .

She was weeping. Clutching her arms inside the sleeves of the faded gown, she walks from room to room in the empty flat. Where are you! London dawn at the grimed net   43 curtains . . . fruit still in the bowl from which, as he finally went, he stole an orange . . . nothing changes and yet everything . . . his smell still on her body . . . And where am I? Snivelling round the debris of you in all the familiar rooms, touching surfaces you touched, taking an orange from the bowl . . . Where am I? Weeping. The ducks don't matter. Do they? Keeping hold on what is, on what exists *after* the shot has echoed and gone, this is all that's important, yes, keeping hold on what I have forced myself to become, with all the sanding and polishing of my heart's hardness, keeping hold of my life alone that nothing – surely not the wounds of one night's loving? – can destroy. So just let me wipe my face on the same washed-out corner of a sleeve. And forget. A stranger carries the dead mallard home, dead smeared heads, bound together with twine. But the sun comes up on the same stretch of river where, only yesterday, they had life . . .

*

Marcus held Anna. They stood by his car. It was still morning, yet they sensed the tiredness in each other, as if neither had slept at all.

'I'll be going then, old thing. Sorry I was such a miserable bugger. Selfish of me to disturb you with my little problems.'

'Oh, you weren't disturbing me.'

'Yes, I was. Typical of me: Marcus Ridley's Lament for Things as They Are.'

44

'I don't mind. And last night –'

'Lovely, Anna. Perhaps I'll stop dreaming about you now.'

'Yes.'

He kissed her cheek and got quickly into the car.

'Good luck with the novel.'

'Oh yes. Thank you, Marcus.'

'I'll picture you working by your river.'

'Come and see the children, Marcus. Please come and see the children.'

'Yes. Alright. No promises. Are you going to work on the book today?'

'No, I don't think I can. Not today.'

'Poor Anna. I've tired you. Never mind. There's always tomorrow.'

'Yes, Marcus,' and very gently she reached out and touched his face, 'there's always tomorrow.'

Words With Marigold

I don't know why me. I don't know why you want to talk to me. I'm no different from anyone. I mean, there are hundreds – thousands – of girls like me, aren't there? Perhaps you're going to talk to us all, are you? Lost Generation, or whatever it is they call us. I've always wondered how they do surveys. I bet they take a tiny sample of people and call it a silent majority. I mean, I bet they can't be bothered to go round asking hundreds of people the same stupid questions. Except I met one on a train once. A survey person. She tried to make me answer things like 'How frequently do you travel on this train?' I said, that's my business, *dearie*, I said I don't own much, but I own what I do and why I do it. She went puce. I followed her down into First Class and she got this group of men in business suits and they invited her to sit down. I suppose it was a great day for them. I suppose they'd been longing for years for someone to ask them what they were doing on that train! They were drinking whiskies an' that. They travelled on that train every day.

I'm not extraordinary though. I suppose it's considered extraordinary to have a termination at sixteen, but I can tell you it isn't, if that's what you're thinking. I mean, it's no more extraordinary than having a fuck. In fact, that's all it is, if you think about it. A screw. With consequences. No one worries about anyone having a screw, less they're real actual kids or something. But try getting a termination at sixteen. I mean the stuff you have to put up with. Fine till they suss your age. I mean, perfectly okay an' that, but then they start on at you. They start implying your whole life could be fucked, like you've screwed your whole personality and your whole chances and you're psychologically damaged. They want to make you start believing these things or they wouldn't just act like that, would they? And the stuff about your parents. They imply your Mum's to blame or something because you're too young to think for yourself. They say things like, 'Was your Mother aware of your relationship?' So I said, no love, my Mum's not aware of any sodding thing these days. She's out of her mind most of the time on Special Brew. And her eyes are going as well – disappearing inside her flesh. She's put on three stone since last year.

But actually that is when things started to get bad. I'd have said I was quite alright, like you know, quite happy till that all began. I was working for my O-levels. Biology was my best subject. Biology and Art, but they said you can't take Art. I was okay at Maths. Not fantastic, you know, but okay. I could have got something like a C or something. Eddie used to help me with Maths. I mean quite a lot. Not just five minutes to get you through your homework, but he'd sit down with me when Mum was getting tea and he used to say, Marigold, you've got this tendency to think in straight lines and what I've got to do is to help you think in circles or spirals. He had a name for this kind of thinking. He was very interesting about it and it really started to help me because I'd tended to think there was always one way or doing something and this was the *meant* way. Because at school they never noticed things like how you were thinking, I mean they didn't have time, did they, but Eddie said he'd make time and he did.

I really enjoyed Maths homework after Eddie started to help me. I'd bring extra work home and you could just hear the teachers thinking God, Marigold Rickards taking extra Maths to do at home! But my results got better. It was terrific seeing the results get good. I mean, let's not exaggerate. I'd never be a mathematician or anything, like I could be a painter probably if I could get into art school and get my technique better. I still think I could be a painter. I mean I haven't lost hope, have I, and I know about one of the medical aspects of people in depressions is they lose hope. They just look into the future and see black or brown or something, just some dark colour and nothing in it. But I don't. I mean, I even write letters to people asking them for money to help me get through art college. I don't get any money back, but I keep writing, don't I, so that must be a good sign. I wrote to Lady Falkender. Someone told me she was a patron of the arts or whatever. Do you think she'll write back or send me something? I mean, I don't know. I can't really imagine how Lady Falkender lives, can you? I don't know if she'd write to someone like me.

I've thought of writing to Eddie, except neither of us – my Mum nor me – know his address. And I bet it wouldn't do any good to write. But it did all start then, when I think about it. Till Eddie left our house I think we were alright. They'd have rows, Eddie and my Mum, but not terrible ones. He never hit her. I mean, don't get me wrong, he wasn't at all a violent person. He liked jokes. He'd make jokes the minute he woke up. Sometimes his jokes got on my wick, but other times I'd think, he kind of keeps us all going and if he weren't here or something we'd probably have nothing to laugh at and we'd just go quiet like I suppose we must have been before. I suppose when I think about it, I dreaded the idea of Eddie leaving us. I mean I knew my Mum would just go to bits, because you could tell what he was to her. There was nothing she wouldn't do for him. He got the works. Best food she could afford, terrific ironing, thermos washed up, cufflinks and stuff at Christmas . . .

It was the age difference, I think. They were about the same age about, but she looked older. I don't blame him. He was with us for seven years and that's quite long, isn't it? I mean, I was nine or nearly nine when he came. And he never said, I don't think he said Marigold's a fucking nuisance and got me palmed off with neighbours. He just accepted me and treated me like his own kid. I mean, better than some fathers are to their kids. Quite a bit better. Like helping me with my Maths I told you about. And other things. They used to go on outings to London and he'd always say, let's take Marigold, she should have the chance to see the big city an' that. His favourite thing in London was the Science Museum. He knew masses about some of the old compasses and chronometers. There was this man who invented a type of chronometer and he was a kind of hero for Eddie. Harrison. I don't know which century he was. Before Nelson, probably.

My Mum wasn't too interested in chronometers, actually. But I don't think it was that. I mean, you wouldn't leave someone because they weren't interested in something, would you? I think it was definitely the other girl he met. She was some sort of secretary at the engineering works where he worked. I only saw her once, but I think she was quite kind of posh an' spoke all terrific an' wore skirts with linings in them. Know the type I mean? She wasn't specially pretty or anything. Not that I could see. But she was lots younger than my Mum. I'd say she was twenty-eight or nine. And I think she hypnotised Eddie by being this different kind of person and he'd come home and start correcting my Mum's grammar. And my Mum got scared. I mean, this was the pitiful thing. She got frightened she'd say things wrong. She *wanted* her grammar to be better, to please Eddie. And food. He bought my Mum a book called French Cooking Explained. She tried to do things from it for a bit till she sussed the flippin' insult in all that. Then she put the book in the oven and the oven caught fire and that was the first time I ever saw Eddie really angry with her. I heard him yelling at her and I came down and the kitchen was covered with white stuff from the extinguisher, and then my Mum rushed past me and up to the toilet and sicked up. I think she knew that was the end with Eddie. I don't think she'd heard about the girl at work by then. But she knew it was all over for her. I mean, you do, I think. Don't you think? One minute you don't know and then another one minute passes and that's the crucial one, like going into a ghost train, know what I mean? Like this one minute is much longer than even longer, darker things like ghost trains. D'you get it? I got it there and then. I could see that was the crucial minute and our lives wouldn't go on like they were.

My Mum blames Eddie. She thinks she's finished now. She's only forty-four. Eddie left some socks and things behind and she burned these in the yard. I started going off her when she did this. Up till then, I'd felt really sorry for her. I'd hear her crying through the wall. I used to make a tray of tea and go and sit on the bed. Waste of time though. She'd just snivel about 'getting even' and I went off her when she'd start on this. 'Cos it's Eddie's life as well as hers, isn't it? Like in my case it's Alan's life as well as mine. Least, that's what I've had to tell myself. No one's got control. You can be a king of somewhere or the head of a billion-pound corporation or whatever and still get clobbered. Only thing is you've got money if you're a king or something or the head of a billion-pound whatsit. So you can go to art college. Providing they'll take you. You don't have to write begging letters to people. And you've got O-levels.

My Maths got terrible. I'd relied on Eddie, hadn't I? I couldn't get myself to think in spirals or whatever. I lost the knack. So I knew I wouldn't get Maths O. Not even a C or something. I could have got biology because my drawings were good, I mean they looked professional and the drawings are half of it with biology: cross-section of the broad bean, mucor heads, habitat of the brown water beetle . . . I don't know about Eng Lit. I might have got it. *As You Like It* we did. Alan told me *As You Like It* is quite an important play, but I kept thinking, I don't know what they're doing exactly.

I think I'm attracted to people who want to help me. Or they're attracted to me. Alan wanted to help me. I went to get my Mum out of the pub one night, 'cos she couldn't move. She was sitting in a corner, sweating. She used to dribble when she got to this state. Dribble and burp and sometimes sick up. Now I can't stand to see a person drunk. Specially her. I run a mile. I can't go near them or touch them. Alan helped me out with her. I got her to bed and Alan stayed. I don't mean he forced himself on me. I mean, what I did was talk. Like I'm talking to you, but better, because I was deeply attracted to Alan. I mean I'd had some boys, Badger Reid from school and Billy Tansley who thought he was Don Juan 'cos he'd got a second-hand Suzuki! But they were for laughs. Rubbish! Alan was older, see. I mean he was a mature man.

He had this cottage. It's called Green End. It's down a track, miles from anything. He thinks the world of it. He says if he lived in town, he'd wind up killing someone. I don't think he likes people. He likes women. He's a very attractive man.

He didn't seduce me or anything. It was five or something in the morning when I shut up talking and he just lay me down where we were in front of the fire in the front room. I was wearing my school skirt and he came all over it so as not to come inside me. He said coming on my skirt was the most exciting sexual experience he'd ever had. Men say these things, don't they? They say things to make you feel special. I mean, I know that now, but I didn't exactly know it then. So I've learned something haven't I? Means it wasn't all just a waste.

Alan had this handmade kiln in his garden. He'd built it himself, brick by brick. It was fate he was in the pub that one night, because he didn't go out hardly ever. He stayed at Green End and did his pottery. He let me make a pot once, but it was rubbish. He had a university degree from Oxbridge. I knew Oxbridge was two places by the time I met Alan, but I used to think they were one place. I don't think my Mum even knows what Oxbridge is! If you said, what's Oxbridge, Mum? she'd say something like stock cubes. Eddie once told me she was ignorant. Eddie said it was sad when young people got older not knowing anything. He tried to make me promise I'd go on to A-levels and get to university if I could. He said qualifications were everything these days.

My Mum got ill that night after Alan came. I had to stay home from school and try to stop her drinking, the doctor said. What a laugh, eh? I had to stop her going out to buy beer. Fat chance. She was down the off-licence soon as she could stand up, then down the pub. She looked like death. Like a suet roly-poly. She wasn't cared, though, was she? An' she never give me a thought, what I'd done for her. I mean, the day Eddie left, she lost interest in me.

Billy Tansley gave me a lift on his bike to Alan's place. Charged me a quid for the ride, greedy little bugger. Nothing's for nothing, he said. Wanted to charge me another quid for promising not to tell where I was, but I wasn't playing. You tell the whole effing street, if you want to, Billy, I said.

Alan got really excited when he saw me arrive. I mean, to have me coming to him and asking him to help me just gave him a gigantic hard-on. I'd put my uniform on again and I'd washed and ironed the skirt and he just grabbed me by the shoulders the minute he saw me and took me into his kitchen and fucked me against his fridge. You could hear bottles or something fall over inside the fridge 'cos we jogged it so hard. And I thought, God, this guy's the most fantastic person. I mean passionate. I mean, I got him really hyped up, you know, like a desperate animal.

He loved cooking, Alan. He made this terrific vegetarian thing for me the first evening I was there. He said I had beautiful breasts. He wanted me to eat his meal with my tits showing. He told me he had dreams of girls like me when he was married. He said they got in the way of normal marital relations. He said actually these dreams had destroyed his marriage.

His bed was really good, not like normal beds. He had Indian hangings on it and the sheets smelled like he'd been waving josticks over them. I really liked that bed. The nights I spent in it were the best of my life. I used to come all the time. I mean, he knew what to do. He'd been married. He wasn't like Billy Tansley or Badger Reid, those babies. And he came masses. After the first times, he didn't bother getting out when he came. He said to come inside me was the realisation of ten years of dreaming.

I don't know why I go on about him, I mean how wonderful he was and everything. I don't know why I'm telling you all these private sexual things. I mean, I should have forgotten him, that's what everyone says. I shouldn't keep letting myself remember. But it's not exactly remembering. I mean, all those things I had with Alan are just *there*, they're still in me if you know what I mean? I still wake up and think, it can't have happened, what did happen. I still sometimes think I'm in that bed and then we'll have this day in front of us, the kind of day when Alan works at his pottery and I'm just there adoring him, like I was his wife or something . . .

It was a long way to school from Green End. I used to bike it on Alan's bike when I felt like it. But I'd gone right off work and off the other girls. I mean, they used to say crap like 'Billy Tansley told us you got a sugar-daddy, Marigold.' And you should have seen the rubbish they were going with! Those schoolboys couldn't make anyone feel like a woman. They couldn't make a *woman* feel like a woman! They were wankers. Didn't know a thing about passion. So I felt superior. Who wouldn't? Only thing I got better at at school was Eng Lit. Alan knew masses about Shakespeare. He knew what everything meant. He explained *As You Like It* to me from beginning to end. No, I got bloody cheesed off with school, though. Bossy teachers. Girls boasting about their spotty blokes. I was ready to give it up, except Alan kept saying just what Eddie had said – got to stick it out at school till you get the exams. And I think they were right. I regret it now that I had to pack it in.

My Mum turned up one day. She looked a bit better, but she wasn't. She's on the booze now an' that's it. I thought, go on, Ma, do the mother bit. Tell your daughter she's filth. Tell her she's sweet sixteen and chucking her life away on a man of thirty-eight. I was wrong, though. She'd just come for a look. Alan made her a cup of tea and I could tell she was watching her grammar. He impressed her alright. She'd never met anyone like him. I think maybe she even fancied him, 'cos she started on about herself, telling him what a beauty she'd been before she got fat. But she disgusted him. He'd seen her that night in the pub. He thought she was awful, the pits. He pushed her out after we'd had the tea and she looked really hurt like as if she wanted to be invited to stay.

I never thought I'd wind up back with her. You bloody learn though, don't you? You think you've got something made. I did. I mean, I had in a way. If I'd been older and known more about everything and if I'd layed off a bit and not been the kind of slave I was to Alan, then he might have, well, you know, fallen in love with me. I don't say he would. I mean, when I think about it, I realise I'm not clever enough for a man like that, and they want more than sex after a while, they want you to know things and recognise famous paintings and understand Shakespeare and decide how you're going to vote and things like that. He liked my drawings, though. He said I could be a good artist if I got a better understanding of why I drew things the way I do. I never thought that aspect was important in drawing, but perhaps it is. If I went to art school, they'd help me with this, wouldn't they? I dunno. Don't suppose I'll ever get there, anyway. You've got to have A-level for art school, haven't you? It's not just a question of the money.

I thought of telling Lady Falkender about the baby. I think I need to talk to someone in a letter or something because quite often I feel clobbered by all that and I start to go down like I am now and not wash or eat or take care of myself. I don't cry. I just think about it and then I get this drained feeling, like being numb and losing touch with gravity or something. I hardly told anyone at the time. I mean, I told Alan because I told him I don't mind having it if it's yours and mine, in fact I'd love to have a little baby and care for it. But he didn't want it. He didn't even want to hear about it and he gave me this long lecture about his wife who spent nine years trying to have a baby and how she came almost to full term twice and then had miscarriages and how she suffered. It was like he hated me for wanting the baby his wife had wanted. He'd gone off me a bit after my Mum came, but now he went off me really. I'd hang around him, hoping we could make love and he'd be like he'd been at the beginning, all hot an' that. I'd put my uniform on and go and kiss him on the mouth and push myself against him. Sometimes we'd fuck, but he didn't kiss me or hold me afterwards. He'd fuck with his eyes shut, like he'd get turned off if he looked at me.

He arranged everything. He got me an appointment with some Pregnancy Advice Group. He said, don't worry, Marigold, I'll see you through the actual abortion. But it was finished by then. He despised me. He thought I was stupid to have got pregnant. He said it was the fault of my upbringing. He said the working classes were still miles behind, specially the women, just stupid and ignorant.

His wife's back with him now. I biked out to see him just the one time when the thing was over, the termination I mean. I suppose I thought, if I can't have his baby, perhaps I can still have him. I don't know what made me think this. You're naive at sixteen, I guess. You hope for things you'll never get, I mean probably never get in your whole lifetime. But I thought, I've done what he wanted, got rid of the baby, so he owes me something. But there was this woman there. Someone about his age or a bit younger. She was ever so slim and she walked like she'd once been a dancer. I hadn't a clue who she was. She just came out and stared at me and said, 'I'm Alan's wife. What do you want?' I could have told her, couldn't I? I mean I could have just given it to her, the nights I'd been there and the baby and those dreams of schoolgirls he'd confessed. I could have let her have it all. But it wouldn't have changed anything. It was like when Eddie left our home. You couldn't have made him change his mind.

And I know I've got to get on now. Look at me. I look terrible, don't I? My Mum says there's a job going at the turkey place where she works an' I ought to try to get it. I hate turkeys and meat of any kind. It's probably gone by now, anyway, the job. And I get depressed about not getting my O-levels. I mean, there was a time when I could have got Maths even, and I can imagine Eddie being ever so pleased and taking us out for a celebration at the Wimpy. I don't feel rancour, though. I mean, like I said, it's Eddie's life, isn't it, and Alan's life and you've got to make the best of what's left. Otherwise you just go down. And I don't want to go down, but I wish Lady Falkender would write to me. I mean, I've got hopes of that 'cos I think she's the kind of person who might understand. I could be wrong though. I've been wrong about a lot of things.

A Note on Rose Tremain

Rose Tremain is the author of *Restoration* and *Sacred Country*. *Restoration* won the *Sunday Express* Book of the Year Award; it was also shortlisted for the Booker Prize and was a bestseller in Britain, America and France. *Sacred Country* won the Prix Femina Etranger and the James Tait Black Memorial Prize.

Her other novels are *Sadler's Birthday*, *Letter to Sister Benedicta*, *The Cupboard* and *The Swimming Pool Season*. She has also published three volumes of short stories, *The Colonel's Daughter* (for which she won the Dylan Thomas Short Story Award), *The Garden of the Villa Mollini* and *Evangelista's Fan*. She has written numerous plays for radio and television, including *Temporary Shelter*, winner of a Giles Cooper award. Her work has been translated into thirteen languages.

Rose Tremain lives in Norfolk and London with the biographer Richard Holmes.